Forevermore

Britt Reign

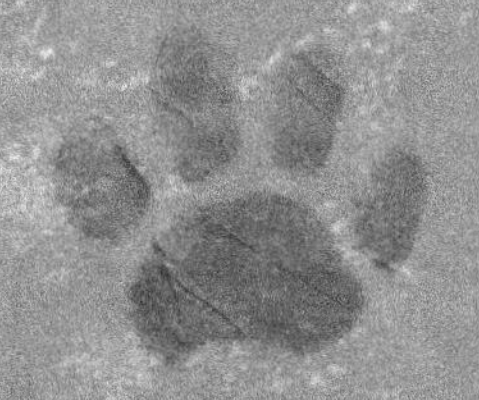

Blurb

The moment their eyes met; she knew she'd been waiting
for him forever.

And it wasn't the first time they met. Just the first time in
this lifetime.

Two lost stars, finding their only lights.

A love so old. It refuses to die.
Even when death tries.

Trigger Warnings:

-Death/Grief

-Depression/Psychosis/Mental Health

-Thoughts of Suicide

-Alcohol/Medication Misuse

-Loss of parent

-Spiritual/Occult themes

-Darker Themes

Tropes

-Fated Soulmates

-Past lives

-Instant Recognition

-Dark Gothic Paranormal Romance

-Supernatural elements

Playlist

1. Euclid – Sleep Token
2. Zombie – YUNGBLUD
3. Panorama Daydream – Ghost Atlas
4. Dangerous – Sleep Token
5. Perfect Soul – Spiritbox
6. The Drug In Me Is Reimagined – Falling In Reverse
7. Only When It's You – Bleeding Verse
8. Past Lives- BØRNS
9. twin flame – mgk
10. Once In A Lifetime – John Michael Howell
11. Your Ghost – SayWeCanFly, DVRKCLOUD
12. Just Pretend – Bad Omens
13. Rain – Sleep Token
14. Everything - Lifehouse
15. Lunacy Fringe – The Used
16. Crows – The Plot In You
17. The Love You Want – Sleep Token
18. Take Me Back To Eden – Sleep Token
19. Eternity – Alex Warren
20. War of Hearts (Acoustic Version) – Ruelle
21. Sleepyhead – Jutes
22. Creature In The Black Night – Dayseeker
23. Limerence – Jutes
24. Taking Over Me – Evanescence
25. Drowning Therapy – Cane Hill
26. Specter – Bad Omens
27. Drown – Bring Me The Horizon
28. Death of Me – Amira Elfeky
29. DIE 4 U – Kami Kehoe
30. iris – mgk, Julia Wolf
31. orpheus – mgk
32. Afterlife – Hailee Steinfeld
33. Forevermore - Atreyu

Prologue

When the other half of you dies.

You will know hollowness.

You will know a profound sorrow, that surpasses the essence of grief.

You will know what it is to be completely and utterly alone.

What it feels to have your entire being split in two.

You will become close friends with the dark.

And the demons that only come out at night.

They call it psychosis.

I call it soul splitting.

After all, our love is forevermore.

1

Hugin

I'm running on the path in the woods behind our house. Rain pours down as lightning cracks in the distance.

Eden is nowhere to be found.

Rushing through the brush of the trees, I can barely make out the branches that whip across my face.

She insisted we still come out tonight to play even though you could smell the impending rain in the air.

Her desire to be hunted always outweighing her rational mind.

"E, where are you?" I yell out for her. My voice barely audible in the heavy downpour.

"Catch me if you can, Hu!" I think I hear her shout out playfully.

A crow caws out and my eyes catch it landing in a tree nearby. I'm distracted for a moment before the faintest glimmer of white catches my eye in the distance. Like a ghost she appears and then is gone again in a blink.

"Baby, come on. Not tonight. We're going to get struck by

lightning!"

"Catch me, Hu!" Eden taunts, her sultry voice closer than it was before.

I see a flicker of white to the left in my periphery.

The sound of Eden's giggles causes shivers down my spine and my feet pick up the pace racing toward her.

Thunder rumbles. It shakes the ground below my feet and dulling the sound of my footsteps as I sneak up on Eden.

Her long, wet, raven hair, whips me across the face as I grab her from behind. Twisting her, I shove her against a tree. Gripping her by the wrists, I pin her arms above her head. My cock getting harder at the sight of the ruby ring on her ring finger. *Mine.*

A yelp and a haunting giggle escapes Eden as I press my hard body against hers, caging her against the tree.

"E, we really shouldn't," I groan, licking the rain off her slender neck. Grinding Eden into the tree, I can't get enough of her.

Eden's fucking intoxicating. The perfect amount of ethereal and unhinged.

"Doesn't the thought of getting struck, make you want to fuck me even harder, Hu? It could be the last time." Eden nips my lip with her teeth, drawing blood.

"Fuck baby, why do you always have to taunt death?" I graze my teeth over her collarbone, drawing blood. Licking up the droplet with my tongue.

Eden melts under my touch.

"You haven't said no yet, Hu. You caught me. Now do with me as you wish," Eden all but begs, grinding against me. Her eyes, hungry, never leaving mine.

Without releasing her arms, I manage to get my pants

down just enough to free my cock that's aching for her.

"That's because I can't tell you no, baby. Life or death, it's always you, E. You're my forevermore," I whisper, before I lift Eden up against the tree and wrap her legs around me. I slide my big hands up under her white slip dress that makes her look like my fucking angel from hell.

"No panties. Fuck, I love when you're ready for me."

I pull her down onto me, plunging deep inside her. Claiming what's mine. Fusing our souls back together.

A tortured moan leaves Eden as her pussy clenches around my cock, before lightning strikes the ground so close to us. Too close. She screams but it's muffled by the sharp crack. A blinding, bright white light is all I see.

2

Hugin

I'm blinded by bright lights that line the ceiling of the hospital when I try to open my eyes at the sound of my dad's voice. I try to shield my eyes with my arm. It's still too bright.

"Son, it's time to wake up. It's time to go," I hear my dad say somberly.

We've been here forever. I must've fallen asleep in my chair.

"What about Mommy, Dad?"

My dad's eyes look so sad. I've never seen him look this sad.

"Hu…" My dad starts but then clears his throat, looking away for a second, before looking back at me. He reaches for my hands and holds them between his. "Hu… Your mom… She's gone and she won't be coming home… Your mom died, Hu. I'm so sorry." My dad pulls me to him and starts crying so hard.

I think I cry too.

I'm sitting in this flower house while Mommy sleeps in front of me.

Mommy looks like a princess. She is surrounded by so many pretty flowers. It's like being in a field full of flowers except indoors.

I move around in my chair a lot. It feels too big for me.

These clothes I'm wearing are itchy but I look like Dad.

Dad is standing talking to people I don't know next to the big fancy box Mommy is sleeping in.

He said she's going to be sleeping for a very long time but I will see her again someday. That she went to heaven to be with the angels and will keep me safe from there.

It's too quiet in here, but I hear people whispering about Mommy and the car accident. I think they think I can't hear them, but I hear everything.

I don't like it here. It smells funny. Everyone looks really sad. No one seems to want to look at me for very long.

I feel like I want to cry but Mommy can't hold me if she's sleeping, so I am trying not to. Mommy is the only one who makes me feel better when I'm sad.

I'm going to miss her making me dinosaur nuggets and smiley face pancakes. Singing to me if I wake up with nightmares. Her singing always helps me fall back to sleep. She sounds like an angel. I wonder if that's why she's an angel now.

"Hu...it's time to say goodbye, bud. They are going to close Mommy's casket now." Dad comes over to take my hand and leads me to the casket.

I watch Mommy sleep. She doesn't move. She doesn't smile. She looks like Mommy but she also doesn't look like Mommy.

"Wake up, Mommy," I whisper, squeezing her hand. Her pretty red ring digs into my hand.

I always loved that ring. It was so shiny. Mommy always said the color red reminded her of a love forged in fire. A flame that refused to die. I never knew what she meant but every time she talked about it, Mommy almost sparkled as much as her pretty ring.

Dad sounds like he's crying behind me. I turn around and look up at him, but his back is turned away from me. His shoulders are shaking.

Turning back around, I take Mommy's ring off of her finger and quickly put it in my jacket pocket.

I feel Dad's fingers gently squeeze my shoulders. I think he saw me take Mommy's ring, but he just says, "It's time to go, bud."

"I'll miss you, Mommy," I whisper, as a tear runs down my cheek. I feel all of the hurt in my chest burst out in a sob.

Dad scoops me up in his arms and carries me to the car. I cry the whole way there.

We are at the cemetery. At least that's what Dad called

it. Dad asked me to sit over by this tree, so he could watch me. He didn't want me to see Mommy's casket going into the ground.

I can still see from here, but I won't tell him that. Dad seems really sad and I don't want to make anything harder for him.

So, I sit under this tree and watch the crow that is sitting on the tree branch above me. We have a staring contest and I lose.

I squeeze Mommy's ring in my pocket. It was special to her, so it will be special to me. Dad never asked me for it back so I don't know if he saw me take it or not.

"Why you sad?" A little girl with long hair the color of the crow, appears from behind the tree, scaring me.

I jump up and cover my mouth. I try not to scream because I feel like I'd get in trouble if I do.

"You scared me!" I whisper.

"I sowwy. You look weally sad. Want hug?" the little girl asks.

"Mommy told me not to talk to strangers."

"I not scawy. I not a stwangah. I dis many." She holds up three tiny fingers.

"You are three years old?"

"Yep! You biggah dan me! I not scawed a you." She smiles.

I walk a little bit closer to her. She seems really nice. "I am six. Wait, why are your eyes two colors?"

"I dunno. Want hug?" she asks again, coming even closer to me.

I watch her for a little bit. The girl dances around the

tree, giggling. Her long hair blows in the wind, with the leaves of the tree. She makes me feel less sad.

"Yeah." I open my arms and she runs and almost tackles me in a fit of giggles.

Her giggling has me laughing softly. I try to be quiet. I don't want to make Dad mad.

A branch cracks on the ground behind me causing me to jump back.

"Son, who are you talking to?" my dad asks.

"What's your..." I turn to ask her, but the little girl is gone.

I look around everywhere but I don't see her anywhere.

How did she disappear so fast?

"It's time to go, Hu." My dad takes my hand and leads me over to the dirt where my mommy is.

I stand still, just looking down at my shoes in the soft grass.

I can't look at the dirt. It makes my chest feel heavy.

Raindrops start to fall from the sky. Landing on my eyelashes.

It's like the sky knows I want to cry.

"Let's go before you get sick, Hu." My dad gently grabs my hand.

I'm not ready but I have to listen to Dad.

"I'll miss you, Mommy," I whisper and hope my words float up to the sky and reach her.

"She miss you too." I hear in that little girl's voice. My eyes look everywhere for her but I can't find her.

Turning to leave, I walk with my dad to the car. We walk past people I've never seen before. I hear them whispering and think someone says, "I can't believe she drowned. It's so tragic."

I wonder what drowned and tragic means.

Dad opens my door to the back seat of the car and there is a small white rectangle on the ground. It looks like the card dad gave me at the flower house Mommy was just at. He said it was for prayers for Mommy and I should keep it somewhere safe.

I must've dropped it. I pick it up and put it in my pocket quick, before getting in the back seat. I check to make sure the ring is still there and it is.

Once Dad gets in the car, he takes a deep breath, shakes his head and starts driving home.

The car ride is so quiet except for the rain that continues to fall the whole way home. Dad doesn't even have the radio on. Every so often I hear him sniffle but I stay quiet.

I fall asleep with my head against the window, squeezing Mommy's ring in my hand.

3

Eden

"Hu?" I gasp awake, sitting up in bed as a crack of lightning flashes through my bedroom window. The echo of Hugin's voice haunts me on a never-ending loop. That's all I hear. It drowns out my own thoughts. My own voice. He is always everywhere and nowhere at the same time.

It's so dark in here, aside from the lightning in the distance. The power's been out for days. At least it feels like days.

Jumping out of bed, I almost lose my balance as a wave of dizziness hits me. I don't even bother steadying myself before I'm rushing to my dressing room.

The second I'm in the room, I'm ripping the dresser drawers out of my vanity. I dig for the ruby ring Hugin gave me all those years ago.

"Where the hell is it!?" I scream, slamming my hand down on the vanity.

I look down at my hand, double checking that it isn't there. It's not.

The light from my kerosene lantern flickers.

"Hu! Is that you?" I yell out.

The light brightens, illuminating the wreckage I created.

"Where is it, Hu?"

All of the drawers and their belongings are thrown and scattered around the large dressing room.

The vanity stool is toppled over on its side.

When I spin around, I notice a glass of red wine sitting on the vanity. Somehow it hasn't toppled over. Reaching for it, I finish it in one gulp. I reach for the bottle to pour more into my glass, only to find it empty.

"Ahhhh!" I scream. Tossing the bottle to the floor.

I go to my closet, grabbing my black satin robe from the clothes rod and wrap myself in it.

Taking off for the stairs, I run down the spiral staircase, through the hallway, into the kitchen, and shove the back door open.

I make a bee line for the garden.

Maybe I dropped the ring there!

I stare up at the ominous sky. Gray and black clouds swirl overhead. The lightning flashes closer now, the storm brewing in the air, waiting to break free.

When was the last time I saw it?

A huge gust of wind blows my robe open. My long black hair whips all around, covering my eyes.

The wind is whistling loudly, angrily. I feel as if my irritation is fueling it.

The air smells damp, earthy, thick. I can feel the electricity.

A flash and then a crack overhead before a heavy downpour falls from the sky.

Thunder rumbles a few seconds later.

The bolt of light the only thing that highlights my path to the garden.

If only I'd be struck by lightning.

"Why do you always tempt death, baby?" I hear Hu ask me.

"Because I hate existing without you."

"We are always one, E. Two halves of the same soul. Forevermore, remember?"

"It isn't the same! You aren't here! I need you here! I'm not supposed to be here without you!" I scream out answering the voice in my head.

"I'm always here."

A sob leaves me at the sound of his voice echoing in my mind. My tears drowned out by the rain that's pouring down, soaking me through my robe. It seems as if the rain falls harder, the harder I cry.

How do you bury someone who still whispers your name in the dark?

Mud squishes under my bare feet.

I can hardly see anything around me, but I could find my way to the garden even if I was sleepwalking.

"Where is my ring?" I shout, throwing my hands in the air, as if the sky will answer me.

I almost slip on the wet grass, just barely catching myself.

The second my toes touch the edge of the garden, there

is another strike of lightning. It hits so close and is so bright, it almost blinds me.

"Strike me! I dare you!" I taunt the sky, laughing maniacally.

Without warning, a black crow swoops down at me, startling me, catching me off balance.

In seconds, I'm slipping and falling.

My skull hits the earth with a thud before I even have time to react.

The last thing I see before I drift off, is a black crow dropping something in front of my eyes, before it flies off into the stormy night sky.

4

Hugin

I'm in my room snuggled up in bed staring up at my glow in the dark stars on my ceiling, when lightning flashes outside my window.

I pull my outer space comforter up over my head and start counting, waiting for the thunder to roar. I'm so afraid of storms.

I hold Mommy's ring tight in my hand.

"Please keep me safe, Mommy," I whisper into the dark.

Thunder rumbles outside. The house shakes and rattles from the wind. My body starts to tremble.

I wish Daddy would let me sleep in his room but he says I'm too big. I have to sleep in my own room.

I don't like storms. They're so loud.

I hear tapping on my window, but I'm too afraid to look.

Mommy used to rub my back and sing to me until I fell asleep when I was scared.

I squeeze my eyes closed tight and start humming. I pretend Mommy is here and singing to me.

I hear the tapping again, so I hum a little louder. Hoping it's just a tree branch scratching my window.

I'm under my covers asleep when I hear the sound of a girl's voice softly singing, *"Somewheh ovew the wainbow, two biwds fwyyyy..."*

Her voice is so comforting, it lulls me into a deeper sleep.

A crash of thunder so loud I feel it in my body, has my eyes flying open. Staring back at me is one blue and one brown eye.

A tiny hand gently holds mine.

I jump up. "How did you?"

But she's gone.

5

Eden

The sky is pitch black, not a single star in the sky when my eyes flutter open. I'm lying in my garden coated in mud.

My skin and clothes are soaked.

My teeth are chattering and my flesh is covered in goose bumps.

But I couldn't care less.

Hugin has been gone for two years and for those two years I've wanted to be gone too.

I don't just mourn Hugin, I feel his ghost every time the wind brushes my skin. The grief of losing him heavy, but his presence heavier.

Every time I dream, he's alive. Waking up, the cruelest kind of mourning and in those moments, I beg the universe to just take me too.

I tempt death every chance I get but she doesn't seem quite ready for me yet.

Hugin took my soul with him when he died. Now all I have left of him is his voice that lives rent free in my head and this garden he built me.

I can never leave. His ashes are scattered amongst these rose bushes.

It's the one thing I continue to tend to, to keep him alive.

It's the only thing that matters to me anymore. The only thing that keeps me alive.

These roses breathe for me, exhaling oxygen like a prayer. The only breath that sustains me, for I imagine it's Hu's soul. His ashes woven into their roots, giving me life with each crimson bloom.

Extending my fingers out, I reach for a red rose, pressing the thorns against my fingertips needing to feel something. To feel anything.

All I ever feel is a perpetual numbness. A deep sense of emptiness. My vessel is such a desolate place without him. As if a part of me died with him that day. And it did, because Hu was the biggest part of me. He was the light to my dark. Loving Hu was what gave life purpose for me. Some days I don't even know how to breathe without him.

I'm always praying that Hugin will come back for me. That he'll take me to whatever realm he left me for. Wishing it was all just a nightmare and I'll just wake up one day and get to see him and touch him again.

It's still deep into the night. The silver glow of the full moon is almost dimmed by the dark clouds of the storm.

I just lie in the mud and let the cold of the earth seep into my bones, as I stare up at the sky.

Raindrops coat my skin, as I watch a lone crow look as if it's flying toward the moon. I wonder why it's alone. Crows are supposed to mate for life, at least that's what Hu always told me.

"Did you lose your mate too?" I yell out, as if it can understand me.

The crow tries to seek refuge from the storm, in one of the oak trees nearby.

His sleek black wings are spread as the wind tries to change his flight direction.

My eyes are transfixed on the elegant creature.

The crow lets out a warning caw before there's a rumble of thunder.

I continue to lie here. Hoping the earth will swallow me whole.

6

Hugin

It's been a couple weeks since Mommy went to heaven. I'm sitting under the same tree with the same crow in the cemetery, as I watch Dad cry over the dirt hole, they put Mommy in.

"Dance wid me pwease?" A sweet voice asks from behind me.

Getting up, I look behind the tree and the little girl with black hair twirls in circles.

"Pwease?" she asks again, dancing all around.

"There isn't any music." I shrug my shoulders. "Wait, where's your mommy?"

"Dunno. How bout wing awound a wosy?" She claps her hands together in excitement, jumping up and down.

The little girl seems so excited I can't tell her no.

"Okay." I hold both of my hands out for her to hold on to.

She squeals and runs over to me. Placing her tiny hands in mine.

We start running in circles. She's like watching the sun

shine, as she sings the song.

Her loud giggles make me laugh.

"We aw faw down!" she yells jumping on me. Knocking both of us over.

I watch Mommy's ring fall out of my pocket and hit the ground; before my head cracks off of a tree root.

The crow caws, the little girls' giggles stop, and my eyes flutter closed.

1

Eden

I'm lying in our garden. When a flash of lightning and another loud caw, that sounds so close, has me fluttering my eyes open.

My head is thumping.

How long have I been out here?

How did I get out here?

I'm shivering violently but I don't care.

It's not even dawn yet. The dark clouds still mute the morning light. Casting the yard in shadows.

The crow sits on Hugin's headstone in the garden, only a foot from my head.

I trace my fingers where I engraved, *'Hugin Orion, eternity keeps us entwined, forevermore.'* The crow never moving.

Rain still pours down from the sky.

Water droplets decorate its wings like pearls.

Our eyes lock and for a moment, I feel a sense of familiarity with the crow.

The crow watches me closely. Its eyes never leaving mine.

When I reach up to touch it, the crow drops something and immediately flies away before my fingers can even trace its delicate wings.

Lightning flickers overhead and illuminates something shiny in the mud.

Reaching over to see what the crow had dropped, sits a gold ring.

Picking it up. I wipe the ring on the sleeve of my black robe.

A gold ruby ring... So similar to mine.

Standing so swiftly, I almost lose my balance as my head swims.

Fighting through the heaviness, I run out of the rain to the back door of our Victorian home.

I don't even bother to wipe my feet in the mudroom before I'm tearing up the spiral staircase to my dressing room.

My clothes are cold as ice, clinging to me but I don't care. My body feels numb anyways.

This room looks like a hurricane blew through it the second I barge through the door.

I dig through the wreckage of my belongings that litter the floor.

I can't find the ring anywhere.

I never take it off except for when I go swimming in the lake. Terrified I will lose it if it slips off. I always store it in the top middle drawer of my vanity. Right next to the sapphire hair comb Hugin's father gave to me as my something old and blue on our wedding day. The same comb Hugin's mother wore on their wedding day.

The gold ruby ring is nowhere to be found.

Turning up the flame of the kerosene lamp on my vanity, I view the ring from the crow more closely.

That's when I see it... 'E&H Forevermore' engraved on the inside of the ring.

How did that crow get this?

Had I lost it in the garden without realizing it?

When was the last time I even wore it?

The ring falls from my hand, when I notice the smallest amount of dried blood that fills the engraved letters to the *Forevermore.*

My ears begin to ring, vision starting to blur. The room feels like it's closing in on me.

A wave of emotion hits me like a tsunami. I hear the ping as the ring hits the hardwood floor before the room goes pitch black.

8

Eden

A hard tapping of wood reverberates throughout the house, notifying us it's time to get into position. I'm hiding in one of the dark, secret passages of Lunalight Lair waiting for our first tour group to walk through, so I can scare the hell out of them.

I crouch down so quietly behind the disappearing panel. Plunged in darkness hidden in the walls, all of my senses on high alert, listening closely for our guests to get close. My long raven hair is tied up in two messy space buns. A luminescent white paint makes my skin look porcelain in the dim light. My eyes are blacked out with contacts, while small black cracks mar my skin showcasing just how broken I am. I'm dressed in a black and white plaid frilly dress that hits just above the knee. My outfit is complete with knee-high white socks and ratty black combat boots. I look fragile, haunted, and unhinged. Just how I like it. Just how I feel inside.

The air smells faintly of fog machine, plywood and must. The slightest hint of gasoline lingers in the air from the masked man with the chainsaw lying in wait not too far into the house from where I'm hiding.

Dim red glow and strobe lights turn shadows into living things as you wander the halls of the lair. Each creak of the floorboards as I occasionally rock back and forth to get into character are drowned out by the muffled soundtrack of distant screams and haunting music.

I get giddy inside, my adrenaline pumping as I prepare to jump out and scare someone.

Sometimes I like to hum low eerie melodies as I stalk our guests. Pop up behind them and laugh maniacally when they least expect it.

They are in my lair after all.

I follow the rules though. We aren't allowed to touch anyone but we can chase them and taunt them, shriek and laugh in their faces. I like to read people's energies, so when I find someone I like, someone who feels uneasy to me, I torment them a little extra.

Some of the other haunters who work here say they leave feeling unsettled sometimes. That they're jumpy when they go home and see a shadow in their own hallway. Their hearts jolt when they forget where some of us are hiding here in this house, even though they know it's all just a fantasy. They've said they never want to leave still in character because it messes with their heads.

But this fuels me. I get off on the thrill of living like I'm inside of a horror movie, just creating my own script. Sometimes I feel like if I stay here long enough, I can convince myself the character I'm playing is actually real.

Or that maybe I'm not playing a character at all.

ootsteps start to slowly pad down the hallway I'm hiding in. I start to sing a haunting melody.

"Bro, it's so hard to see with the fog and these strobe lights," a guy says right in front of my panel.

That's my cue.

Slamming my panel door down as violently as I can to startle them, I slip out and let out a loud shriek. "That's the point. We don't want you to see us until it's too late."

Three of the girls and two of the guys in the group of seven yell and jump back.

I let out a high pitched, disturbing laugh and start to crawl toward them like the girl from *The Ring*. Contorting my body in weird angles so I look like a deranged doll.

One lone guy closes out the group toward the end. He's the only one not coupled off and he looks almost unphased by everything.

That fucking infuriates me.

I follow him like a specter. When I get close to his ear I breathe heavily and whisper, "Shh... They'll hear us breathing!"

Nothing. His stoic facial expression doesn't budge.

Slithering down the walls close to their group but staying just out of sight. I jump out and stomp, screaming in agony, "Don't leave me here!"

"Goodness!" one of the girls shrieks, but still not even a flinch from this guy.

I sneak up behind him and slam my hand off of a panel near his head. "They said I'd be safe here... They lied!"

"I'm so sorry!" One of the girls almost hiccups.

I laugh so insanely at her response, that I sound like I belong in an asylum from the 1900s.

I continue to slip through hidden panels and pop out again directly in front of them. "Do you hear it too? The screaming under the floorboards..."

"Make it stop! Make the screaming stop!" I pull at my hair.

This man! Just keeps walking. Every single person in his group I've gotten at least once, but not him.

I'm pissed. I decide to climb up into the rafters and jump down directly in front of him shrieking, "You shouldn't have come! Now you can't leave!"

And yet this guy never bats a fucking eye.

How fucking dare he!

I am so furious I follow him out of the haunted house completely breaking character.

The second we make it out of the exit door; I go to speak but his friends just keep walking. I listen to them talking about how awesome it was. The one girl walks into a cornstalk and accidentally scares herself, jumping into her boyfriend's arms and then laughing hysterically when she realizes it was just a cornstalk.

I notice he stays back from the group though, halting completely in his tracks. When he whips around, he pierces me with a stare so heated I am eviscerated and feel as if I become one with the fog. It's almost like he felt me there.

All of the oxygen leaves me when his deep chocolate brown eyes meet mine. They're so warm. So...familiar. But I can't get distracted by beautiful eyes.

"Why the fuck weren't you scared?" I blurt out way more aggressively than is necessary.

"Excuse me?" he asks, confused but not flinching at my outburst.

"You weren't scared! At all! I did everything I could possibly think of to scare you and you never even flinched. My job is to scare you and you weren't even scared. What the hell!" I go off on him.

"It's all fake. I know it's fake. Why would I be scared?"

"Everyone knows it's fake! It's the thrill! People come here to get their hearts racing. The adrenaline pumping. Just because it's fake doesn't mean people don't get jump scared when something or someone comes at them that they weren't expecting. I can get at least one scream or jump out of everyone, but not you. Why not you?" I all but growl.

"You clearly are very passionate about this and take it very seriously. I'm sorry I offended you by not being scared. I just...wasn't." He shrugs so nonchalantly.

I huff. Exasperated at this man. For being so...so... rational.

"Well, have a great night! Don't come to haunted houses if you aren't coming to be scared! It takes the fun out of it for us!" I turn around almost stomping and head back toward the door.

"Wait... What's your name?" he asks. His smooth voice halting my retreat.

"What?"

"What is your name? I'm Hugin."

"My name... You want to know my name?" I ask confused.

"Yeah... Why not?"

"Um... I don't know. I just screamed in your face for fun and then again because you're infuriating. Why would you want to know my name?"

"Who doesn't love a passionate woman?"

"Passionate... More like unhinged..."

"Tom-a-to. Tom-ah-to. What's your name, Luna?"

"Luna?" I question, even more confused.

"You're hauntingly beautiful, like the moon, and well the name of this place," Hugin says almost shyly.

"No one's ever given me a nickname before..." I start to say.

The door to the haunted house slams open and Edwin, my manager yells for me. "Eden, get your ass back to work!"

I turn around to say goodbye to Hugin but he's nowhere to be found.

Walking back toward the door to the haunted house, I swing the door open and a beautiful crow lands on the top of the doorframe. I stare at the elegant being for just a moment before it caws.

"Go on, shoo," I say softly, gently starting to pull the door closed.

Its wings open like it's going to fly away and I notice it's holding something in his claws.

"What do you have there?" I reach up to see what it's holding, startling the crow, it flies away so quickly it drops the trinket it was carrying.

A ruby ring falls into the palm of my hand.

I stare at the ring in complete awe. It's stunning. I've never held anything this beautiful before.

Where did this come from?

Slipping it onto my right ring finger, I close the door of the haunted house behind me. The sound of screams soothing my own demons, as I'm plunged into darkness.

9

Eden

Hugin and I lie in comfortable silence, in the back of his pickup truck. We're tucked into a sleeping bag, our legs intertwined.

I feel the steady beat of his heart beneath where my hand rests on his chest.

I sigh in contentment. There is nowhere else I'd rather be.

Hugin is my peace in a world where I have only ever known chaos.

The full moon's silvery glow gently bathes us in the only light for miles. Casting an ethereal glow over the open field.

Creating soft, dancing shadows over the grassy expanse surrounding us.

It reminds me of the time when I used to chase shadows through the hallways of the Lunalight Lair. It feels like a lifetime ago.

The night sky is so clear and glittered with stars. I can make out The Milky Way and The Little Dipper perfectly.

It's magical. Serene.

There's a tranquil stillness to the night, not even a rustling of wind through the trees.

I can just barely make out the distant sound of water trickling down stream, from the creek on the property.

"It's so beautiful out here. I could stay here forever," I whisper not wanting to disrupt the sanctuary of peace surrounding us.

"What if we can?" Hugin kisses my hair.

Leaning to look up at him I ask, "What do you mean?"

"It's ours, E. I signed the paperwork for it this morning."

"Really? It's ours? All of this land? That beautiful home?" I ask in awe, pointing toward the old Victorian home that feels like acres away but is still somehow a part of this land.

"It is. As long as you're happy here? As long as you want this too?" Hugin questions, his eyes never leaving mine.

"As long as I'm with you, I'm happy, Hu. You're the only thing that matters. But this place is a dream. I'd love to call it home with you." I gently kiss his lips and nestle in closer to his chest.

This man, this home, is mine. Sometimes I feel like I jumped through a portal of darkness and swam and swam for miles until I finally found my light, my true love, in Hu. Butterflies swarm in my belly at the love I have for this man.

"You are my home, Eden. Forevermore, remember?" Hugin murmurs into my hair, gently running his fingers down my arm until he locks his fingers with mine. Our laced hands rest on his waist, just below his mom's ruby ring, that dangles from a gold chain around Hugin's neck.

I know how much this ring means to Hugin. He told me how he slipped it off of his mother's finger the day she was buried because he needed to keep a piece of her close to him. We still aren't sure how that crow had it at Lunalight Lair two years ago when we met. Hu said crows like to collect trinkets for their mates but I'd like to think that maybe it was the universe's way of bringing us together or maybe his mom's.

All I know is that crow helped me find my mate and I'll never forget the pull I felt toward Hu from the moment our eyes met the day he came looking for the ring.

Pulling into the parking lot of Lunalight Lair, the parking lot is still fairly empty. I usually get here a little bit earlier so I can finish getting ready in my car. I can't drive in those contacts because they make everything dark.

I'm putting my contact in my right eye when there's a knock on my window.

Looking out of my periphery I notice it's the gorgeous man from the other night. Hugin was his name. He's even more stunning in the soft golden hour sunlight. Almost vampiric looking, jet-black hair and warm coffee-colored eyes, well over six feet tall and lean fit, like a swimmer. My eyes take in every inch of him. Thankfully, he probably can't tell how much I'm salivating over him with my eyes blacked out like this.

"Uhh..." Hugin scratches the back of his head. "I know you asked me kindly not to return but I lost something...really important to me. I feel like it might be a lost cause but I wanted to stop by before it got too busy to ask around."

He looks so distressed it splinters my heart the slightest bit.

And my heart is as black as this man's hair so it's unusual for me to feel, well, anything.

I roll my window down. "What did you lose?"

"My mother's ring…"

My heart sinks but then inflates just as quickly. I haven't taken this ring off since I found it. It's such a beautiful ring but I can't keep it if it's a family heirloom. I don't have anything that belonged to my mom. I could never keep this.

"Can you describe it to me?" I ask. Just double checking it's what I found before just handing this gem over.

"It was my mother's… She died…when I was young…" Hugin looks away from me.

Sadness oozes off of him in waves and I feel it in my core. My chest aches for this man and I don't even know him.

Shaking off the sadness, he continues, "It's a gold band with a red ruby. It's all I have left of her. I can't believe I lost it." Hugin runs his hand through his hair, disheveling it.

And HOLY SHIT. I have never wanted to run my hands through a man's hair in my life until this very moment.

I have felt dead inside my entire eighteen years of living but there's something stirring to life inside me just looking at Hugin. Something I've never felt before.

Reaching out my window with my right hand, I place my hand on his cheek.

"It's yours, Hugin."

"What's…?" He stalls when he places his hand over mine and feels the ring on my right ring finger.

I expect him to rip my hand away and pull the ring off. But Hugin gently takes my hand in his and just stares at the ring.

"How did you…?"

"Honestly, you'd never believe me if I told you."

"*Try me.*"

"*A crow had it... Dropped it when I was closing the door to the house last night and I caught it. I didn't even think I just put it on my hand and went back to work. For some reason I haven't wanted to take it off though. I constantly catch myself staring at it.*"

"*Those peculiar creatures love trinkets; so, I actually believe that. My chain must have broken in the haunted house somehow. I usually wear it around my neck. But that pull you feel toward the ring, was sort of how I remember feeling when I saw it on my mother's hand. They were getting ready to close her casket and my father wasn't looking. It was like it was screaming at me to take it. So, I did.*"

"*I'm really sorry you lost your mom. I lost mine too. But I'm glad you kept the ring. It's really beautiful, Hugin.*"

"*I'm really sorry too, Little Luna.*" His eyes soften at my admission.

"*My name's Eden by the way.*" I try to change the subject. I'm never comfortable talking about my mom. It's always made me feel as if her death is on my hands because I lived and she didn't.

"*Eden, it suits you,*" Hugin says, kissing the ring on my finger and gently sliding it off. "*Can I repay you for keeping it safe by taking you to dinner?*"

"*I work tonight.*"

"*That wasn't a no.*" Hugin smirks.

"*When's your birthday?*"

"*Uhh... November third... Why?*" Hugin tilts his head questioningly.

"*I don't work tomorrow night,*" I offer.

"I'm so confused..." Hugin scratches his head.

"You're a Scorpio."

"I'm sorry, Luna, I'm still confused." Hugin chuckles.

His chuckle is so deep, it makes my toes curl. What on earth!

"March eleventh... I'm a Pisces." I smirk.

"Ahh... I got it. I never really got into the astrology thing but I'm guessing that means we're compatible if you're saying yes."

"Yes. Very compatible. Both water signs, intuitive, passionate, emotional, and ironically mirrored birthdays," I rattle off, not even thinking how weird I must look.

"What do you mean mirrored... Ohh... Eleven three and three eleven... Interesting. I'll take your word for it, Little Luna." Hugin smiles warmly at me.

The way that my chest feels when this man looks at me... like I'm not strange... I wonder what his moon sign is. He's so... grounded. I've never met someone who feels so...steady. His energy never wavers.

Hugin must notice my brain has short-circuited. "So, tomorrow night then? I can pick you up here around seven."

"Oooh! It's a full moon!"

"Tonight or tomorrow?" Hu asks.

"Tomorrow..."

Hugin watches me closely. "So...plan something outside?"

"Ahh... You're already too good for me, Hu. But yes, please." I smile at his understanding of me.

"See you then, Lu." Hugin winks, before turning and walking back to his car.

"See you, Hu."

What on earth is this fluttering of wings beating light against my ribs?

We're still laying in the back of the truck wrapped up in each other in comfortable silence.

Those butterflies haven't stopped burning sunrises in my belly since the day I met Hu.

Hugin breaks the silence. "I know you're still young but have you ever thought about getting married?"

"I'm not that young, Hu. I'm twenty."

"I know but I'm twenty-six, E and I am ready but I don't want to rush you into anything. I want you to be certain. You've endured a lot in your short life. My love for you is not going to fade whether we wait or not. I just want to make sure this is something we talk about because I do want to marry you someday, if you want that too."

"Honestly, Hu, before you, I never even thought about it. I always felt like I was born a burden. But I can't picture a world in which you aren't in my life, so yes, I would marry you. It's only ever going to be you for me. I'm just not so sure I'd want a wedding since I don't have any family."

"You are not a burden. Have never and will never be a burden, E. Please don't say that." Hugin kisses the top of my head.

"Maybe not to you, but I was. I never fit in anywhere, Hu. You know that I believe my soul took a leap of faith to come to earth to become a little light being but was snuffed out the second I was born, when my mama died giving birth to me.

I was meant to be the sun but was born a dark cloud instead and I've been a dark cloud until you became my sunny days."

"And you became all of my nights and days, my Luna." Hugin sits up and unclasps the chain around his neck.

Hugin kneels in front of me with the same ruby ring that landed in the palm of my hand two years ago. I sit across from him in the truck bed, smiling in awe at this beautiful man I get to call mine.

"Eden, our love has always felt as if it was written by the cosmos, timeless and infinite. So tonight, under the same stars that brought us together, will you do me the honor of spending this lifetime and every lifetime with me? Finding each other and choosing each other over and over again, forevermore?"

"You have felt like my twin flame from a past life from our very first date, Hu. Yes. Forevermore, I'm yours." My heart beats slow and steady, knowing that Hu is the one for me. Not a single doubt in my mind. If I am a raging sea, he is my steady shore. Our love is deeper than any ocean.

"I got it engraved, so it felt more like ours, than my mother's." Hugin shows me the 'E&H Forevermore' on the inner side of the ring before he slips it onto my left ring finger.

"My mom told me that the ruby signified a love forged in fire when I was little and I had no idea what that meant until I met you. I once read that rubies are embers that burn with devotion, desire, and the ache for eternity. Now you will carry my heart, bound in gold, with you for eternity."

Hugin pulls me in for a kiss and I feel our souls lock into orbit together as one, the second his lips collide with mine. Every kiss with Hu feels as if we've kissed in every lifetime.

Perfectly in sync, soul recognition. Like starlight glimmers across my skin after being trapped in the darkest hell. Our lips touch and a fire ignites, our souls entwine, two celestial bodies unite after lifetimes of drifting apart. I am him and he is me. We are only ever one when it's us. Everything around us dissolves and it's always just us. As if the universe conspired for us to find each other again in this lifetime.

Proof that for one eternal moment, everything is perfectly aligned.

10

Eden

I wake to the soft light of dawn pouring in from the window, above my vanity.

Gods my back aches. I groan in agony.

My eyes blink slowly to adjust to the morning light.

Oof... My head is screaming.

I go to drape my arm over my eyes when I notice dark wings spanned wide, drying. A crow sits perched on the balcony ledge outside.

Staring at the crow, I start to realize my clothes are soaked through. Looking down I realize they're also covered in mud.

My reflection in the door reveals my hair is also matted to the side of my head. Dried dirt crumbles to the floor as I try to rake my fingers through it.

Was I outside? How did I get there? How did I get here?

The ring lies next to my head.

I haven't seen it...since the hospital...

Getting up from the floor, I rush to the French doors leading to the balcony, to interrogate the crow. I lose my balance as the room seems to tip on its access. Falling against the doors, I shove them open harder than I planned. "Did you steal my ring!"

Except the crow isn't there...

Bent over, I laugh almost hysterically. I feel like I'm losing my fucking mind.

"Loneliness will sit over our roofs with brooding wings," I mutter and let the wind carry my words. A line from *Dracula* by Bram Stoker that I've never been able to forget. It rings so true in my life. I was lonely every day of my life until I met Hugin. Now, loneliness haunts me like a creature of the night without him.

11

Eden

$\mathcal{A}$ warm fire crackles in the fireplace of the cabin, giving off a cherry wood aroma.

This place is so quaint. Just a cozy little studio with a gorgeous stone fireplace and a floor to ceiling window where we can view the forest for miles.

Hugin and I are wrapped up in several throws as I lie between his legs on the couch.

He reads *Dracula* to me, his comfort book. I love when he reads to me. His voice soothes all of the demons in my head.

"What's your absolute favorite quote from this book?" I ask, my eyes fluttering closed as Hugin gently runs his fingers through my hair, almost making me fall asleep. I soak up the warmth of him.

"Hmm... I think, 'No man knows, till he experiences it, what it is to feel his own lifeblood drawn away into the veins of the woman he loves.' I always read that line and hoped I'd find a love like that. Then when I learned that my mom's ruby also meant eternal love and was the color of blood,

I knew that when I met the one, I would give her my own lifeblood."

Leaning forward, Hugin grazes his lips against my ear, nipping it and then kissing it. "That's how I knew you were the one for me."

"How?" I barely croak out. My heart in my throat for this man.

Tilting my head up to face him, Hugin catches my lips in a fervent kiss. Breaking it, he rasps, "Because I would sacrifice myself for you in every lifetime, drain myself of blood to give you life, if it meant saving you. There isn't another soul on this planet I would do that for, Eden."

"My soul will always choose you, Hu. Always. I feel bound to you in a way that feels almost freeing." I crawl up his lap and try to straddle him but Hugin hops up and lays one of the throws in front of the fireplace.

Hugin lies down on top of the throw. "Come here, my Eden."

Sauntering over to him, I slowly kneel on the floor, our eyes meeting for a breathless moment. I crawl up his body to straddle his waist. Hugin's body is so warm and hard underneath my soft thighs. I tug another blanket from the couch and cocoon us inside it.

Hugin's fingers trail up my chest, lingering at my throat before guiding my lips to his. His kiss is consuming; dark fire meeting dark fire. My breath falters as he deepens it, his hands threading into my hair, pulling me closer as if he might tether me to his soul.

When his mouth abandons mine, it's only to haunt the hollow of my throat. His lips wander down my neck, grazing, nipping, savoring, leaving my skin alive with heat. His hold tightens around me as he pulls me closer, our bodies pressing together in a rhythm that makes the world fall away. Every touch is a brand, every brush of his lips a promise that feels older than time.

My name falls from him in a growl, rough and aching. I shiver as if the heat from the fire crackling and his mouth aren't scorching my skin.

"Hugin..." My voice trembles, half moan, half prayer. His answering growl vibrates against my skin, low and possessive.

The air thickens, charged, as if the room itself is holding its breath. Firelight dances against the timber walls of the cabin, shadows stretching long as if to watch us.

His hands explore my body with reverence and hunger, mapping every curve of me. His fingers wrap around my hips, digging into my skin as he grinds me down on his cock.

"Lu..." Hugin growls when he notices I'm already bare for him under my red satin chemise. "Such a fuckin' good girl for me."

Hugin lifts me by the waist and drags me up over his chest to his mouth. The first swipe of his tongue on my clit has my thighs clenching tight around his head. My eyes rolling back at the heat of his mouth on me.

Hugin groans. "You taste so fuckin good, E."

I try to grind on his face, but his grip on me is tight, in control. Hugin guides my every movement until I'm lost to him completely. He worships my pussy like it's his own personal altar.

My orgasm is right there, when he stops abruptly, and

nips and sucks my inner thigh.

"Hu... I was so close..." I whine.

"I know, baby. I'm sorry. I'm greedy. I need to feel you come around my cock."

Hugin slides me down his body and lifts his hips with my legs still wrapped around him. I tug his flannel pants down just enough that his cock springs free.

Our eyes meet and the look he gives me sets me on fire. Licking my lips, I grin deviously, before I let my spit dribble down my chin and fall onto the head of his cock.

Hugin groans and thrusts up, his cock sliding against my clit causing me to moan. I'm soaked for him. So needy for him.

He grips my hips and lifts me effortlessly; the sight of his forearm veins pulsing makes me even hungrier for him. So painfully slow Hugin lowers my aching center down onto his throbbing cock. My pussy grips his cock in a vise, as he stretches every inch of me until he's seated deep inside me. I shudder, overwhelmed by the fullness but completely consumed by him.

Hugin's hands never leave my hips as I rock back and forth on his cock. My nails dig into his chest, as I make circles with my hips like I'm grinding a sensual slow dance on his lap, with his cock buried deep inside me.

Hugin's hand leaves my hip. He trails his fingers up my chest and then grips me around my throat. He grins devilishly as he takes over pumping up harder into me. His grip is almost bruising, possessive.

My body feels like it's on fire. I'm so fucking close I could scream. The way his body perfectly massages my clit while he takes my breath away has me seeing stars.

"Come for me, baby," Hugin growls, thrusting up one last time before he reaches his climax with me.

Shattering around him, I gasp, "Hugin."

My eyes fly wide. I can't breathe. I claw at my mouth, my throat, something is jammed inside me, choking me.

My chest heaves, nothing. No air.

Where am I?

Beeping. Relentless, shrill beeping.

Too loud—make it stop.

My nose stings. Chemicals. Antiseptic. Hospital.

"Mrs. Orion. Please, try to calm down. You have a tube in your throat. We can take it out, but you need to stay calm," a woman says.

Panic slams through me.

Why can't I breathe?

"Mrs. Orion, I'm giving you something to help you relax," she says again.

Numbness creeps over me. My body feels heavy, unresponsive. My eyelids flutter like broken wings.

White light sears down from above. My skull throbs with my heartbeat.

That cursed beeping drills into me again, I want to cover my ears but I can't move.

"Mrs. Orion. We're going to remove your intubation

tube now," a man's voice rumbles, muffled, as if underwater.

Pressure in my throat. My chest burns.

"Hugin," I croak, or think I do.

Shadows of bodies move around me, hands working, but I can't tell what they're doing. My limbs won't obey me.

"Mrs. Orion, try to take a few breaths," the man urges.

I think I do. Maybe.

"That's it. Deep breaths," the woman encourages.

A bright light flashes in my eyes. Too sharp, too much, I can't stop blinking.

A needle prick in my toe. I twitch. Another in the other foot. I twitch again.

"She has full sensation. Pupils tracking. Mrs. Orion is breathing on her own," the man reports, while the woman scribbles quickly beside him.

"Where...?" I croak, my voice shredded, barely more than air. My throat burns raw, my head pounds with each heartbeat.

The room tilts, or maybe I'm the one spinning. I can't tell.

Hands lift me gently into a sitting position. A woman presses a cup with a straw to my lips.

"Small sips," she coaxes softly.

Cool water slips down my throat, soothing the fire. I take another, greedier gulp before she pulls it away.

"Where am I...?" My voice rasps, frayed.

"Do you remember anything, Mrs. Orion?" the woman asks carefully.

"I... I was at a cabin. With my husband. Our anniversary..." My chest tightens. "Where is Hugin?"

Something in her eyes flickers, sorrow. She sets the cup aside. "Let me get the doctor, ma'am."

"Doctor? Am I...? How long...?"

"Four weeks, ma'am. I'll be right back..." Her words trail, already fading.

Moments later, the man from before enters with her.

"Mrs. Orion," he says gently. "I'm Dr. Edgar, and this is Nurse Iris. Can you tell me what you remember?"

I swallow, the ache in my throat sharp. "Only...the cabin. With my husband."

Dr. Edgar's voice lowers. "Do you remember the car accident?"

I try to shake my head, but pain explodes through my skull, crushing. "What accident?"

"You and your husband were in a severe car accident. You've been in a coma for four weeks. You were in critical condition when you arrived. The folks who own the cabin called emergency services when you and your husband never checked-in. They told authorities they weren't able to reach you and were worried the storm may have interfered with your travels. Your vehicle was found in a ravine."

My breath stutters. "Where is Hugin?" My eyes search frantically, though my vision blurs with the effort.

The nurse moves closer, taking my trembling hand. My gaze catches on the ruby ring circling my finger, stained with dried blood.

Dr. Edgar exhales, his voice heavy with finality. "I'm so

sorry, Mrs. Orion. Your husband was pronounced dead at the scene."

The world shatters. A scream tears itself from me, raw and feral. My hands rip at the IV lines, desperate to tear them free.

"Mrs. Orion, please," Dr. Edgar murmurs, trying to restrain me without force.

"No! No, no, no! Hugin isn't dead! We were at the cabin, he isn't dead! You're lying!" My sobs rip out of me, guttural, soul-splitting. "I would feel it if he was gone!"

Nurse Iris slips a syringe into my IV. Cold floods my veins. The fluorescent world fractures, fading into sudden, merciful dark.

12

Hugin

Eden and I are driving through the winding Smoky Mountains to a quaint little cabin for our anniversary.

A thick mist hugs the towering trees.

It would be beautiful, if it wasn't so eerie.

We can barely make out our headlights through the fog as it blankets the forest.

The heavy downpour is like a drumming sound on the windshield, obscuring our view even more.

Our windshield wipers can barely keep up with the rainfall.

Eden and I are silent as I try to slowly weave through each twisting bend in the road with minimal visibility.

Lightning strikes, illuminating the road ahead just barely giving us more visualization of where to turn and when to keep straight.

The sound of thunder rumbles throughout the mountain, reverberating off the cliffs, almost shaking the car with its raw power.

The fog only continues to get denser the further into the valley we go.

Rolling down the window, Eden peaks her head out.

"What are you doing? Get your head back in here, Eden! You're going to get yourself killed!" I demand, breaking the silence.

The air smells fresh and damp. The energy feels charged, almost electric.

"I was just trying to see if I could see any better. Relax!" Eden sits back, rolling her window back up.

Our tires skid when we go around a bend, the roads getting slicker from the heavy accumulation.

I'm white-knuckling the steering wheel, barely going twenty miles per hour.

"Baby, please. I just don't want anything to happen to you. We can't even see a foot in front of the car. What if a branch had been sticking out in the road?" I say, concerned.

"I'm sorry. I didn't think about that. I won't do it again," Eden promises, reaching over and gently squeezing my thigh.

I lace my hand with hers. Bringing her hand to my lips and kissing it gently.

"I love you. I just don't want anything to happen to you."

"I love you, for always." Eden leans her head on my shoulder.

In seconds, the car slides. I release her hand and grab the steering wheel with both hands to try to correct it but it's too late.

We're hydroplaning.

Our tires are screeching against the slick asphalt.

Our pickup truck fishtails. I try to turn the steering wheel back, but we just swerve wildly to the right, before we're going over a cliff into a ravine.

Time seems to stop as the car tumbles through the air.

The roar of the engine drowned out by the thunder and rainfall.

The car scraping against tree branches and rocks on its way down.

"I love you, forevermore, Eden. I'm so sorry." My voice cracks in anguish.

"Don't say that!" Is that last thing I hear Eden scream, before we hit the ground with a sickening thud and screeching of metal.

Everything goes black.

13

Hugin

*I*t's a gray, heavy Sunday afternoon. Eden slipped out hours ago. At first, I told myself she just needed space, but the longer she's gone, the more unease coils in my chest.

I climb into my black pickup and take the road that winds toward the lake.

She's been impossibly quiet these last few days, trapped somewhere deep inside herself. Eden gets like this sometimes: distant, unreachable, as if I'm sharing the house with a ghost. But she always comes back. Sometimes after a few hours, sometimes days. She always comes back.

When I finally find her, she's perched on the edge of the old bridge, dropping rocks into the dark water below.

I sit down beside her, close enough to be there but not close enough to startle her. Out of the corner of my eye, I watch her.

"How deep do you think the water is?" she asks suddenly, voice soft, gaze fixed on the lake.

"Not sure... Fifteen, maybe twenty feet," I answer,

turning to face her fully. Her eyes are dulled, far away, like the light's been drained from them. "Why?"

Her voice drops to a whisper. "Sometimes I just get the urge to jump... Just to see what would happen."

The creek behind our house winds all the way here. Eden usually runs the path, then dives in to swim when she's lost in her head. She's always been drawn to water—she used to laugh and say it was the Pisces in her. But I've never found her sitting still on the bridge.

"Baby... Don't ever say that," I murmur, my chest aching. "If you died, it would bury my heart in the ground with you."

Silence. The kind that presses heavy, like the air before a storm.

"If I jumped...would you jump with me?" she asks at last, hesitant, still not looking at me.

"Every time," I whisper back. "You know that. I'd follow you anywhere. But please." My throat tightens. "I'm begging you. Don't jump."

Eden climbs onto the ledge, balancing on the narrow edge of the bridge.

"Baby! Please, sit back down!" My voice cracks with panic.

"Jump with me," she dares, extending her hand toward me, the sun glinting off the ruby on her finger.

"E...please, get down from there," I beg, every word careful, as though too much urgency might push her over.

"You said you'd do anything for me," Eden whispers, and then she steps off the edge.

My heart stops.

Instinct takes over. I snatch up a heavy stone from the ground and hurl it into the water, praying it might break the surface for her. Without hesitation, I scramble onto the ledge and dive after her.

The moment I hit the water, the world shatters into ice. The breath rips from my lungs. For an instant, everything is silence, darkness, stillness.

*P*ing... Ping... Ping...

I wake to the sound of rain hammering against twisted metal, thunder growling overhead.

Cold. My body is frozen stiff, teeth rattling as I hang suspended, trapped upside down by my seat belt. My skull pounds, vision swimming.

A crack of lightning slashes through the shattered window and that's when I see her.

Eden. Hanging beside me, upside down, still and lifeless.

Blood snakes down her temple from a deep cut, her skin drained of all warmth.

"Baby..." The word tears out of me, broken.

I try to move, to reach for her, but my body won't obey. No sensation below my neck. Paralyzed. Helpless.

"Please...open your eyes..." I choke, voice breaking into sobs.

Lightning flashes again.

And in that violent burst of white, I see black wings unfurled, filling the space behind her like a shadow.

My breath catches as a crow's gaze meets mine through the cracked glass.

"P-please..." I stammer, blood bubbling in my throat. "S-save her..."

Thunder booms. A raw, anguished caw splits the night and then everything goes dark as my body gives out and I release my final breath.

14

Eden

*I'*m paralyzed as my body plunges into the ice-cold water. Inhaling sharply, I ingest a mouth full of water. I feel my lungs start to fill. My chest burns.

The funny thing is, I actually can't swim, but I never told Hugin that.

There's a part of me that's always wondered what it would feel like to drown. I've never understood why that thought pops in my head so often.

I typically just come out here and sit along the shoreline off the trail from our house up to my knees in water. It recenters me enough that I don't actually have to swim in it. Occasionally, I feel the pull of the water and test myself, seeing how deep I'll allow myself to go before rationalizing that it's a bad idea being out here alone.

I never learned how to swim because no one ever taught me the things kids are supposed to be taught by their parents. My aunt never wanted children, but she took me in after my mother died. Never knowing who my father was but loving her sister enough, my mom, that she didn't want her child to end up in and out of foster homes. My aunt wasn't the nurturing type. She made sure I had clean clothes, was fed and had a roof over my head but that was as far as her "love" extended toward me.

Once I met Hu and moved in with him, she essentially sent me on my way with the number of things I owned filling two duffel bags. They fit perfectly in the trunk of the beater car she gave me when I turned sixteen.

It's so peaceful down here.

I stare up where the light hits the top of the water. The sunlight causes the surface to shimmer like a mirror ball, sunlight dancing and scattering, as the water gently ripples to its melody. My mind is finally quiet. I am present in this moment. Lost in how beautiful the water shimmers, like liquid glass, as I sink further and further into the darkness.

Hugin's face is the last thing I see swimming toward me before I succumb to the abyss.

*M*y eyes snap open. Inhaling sharply, I sit up in the bathtub.

My empty glass of red wine and bottle of Seroquel sit on the edge of the tub.

Immediately my eyes search for the ruby ring.

There it sits on my left ring finger on top of my gold wedding band.

Twisting my head, when I hear a caw. I catch the tail of black feathers through the small window above my tub.

I almost slip, jumping out of the tub.

Ripping a towel off of the back of the door, I wrap myself in it. I run out of the bathroom, down the hallway, coasting down the stairs, to the backyard.

I spin in circles looking for the crow but I can't spot him anywhere.

Looking up at my bedroom window, there's a shadow of a man with midnight black, disheveled hair, standing with his back to my window. His edges almost appear blurred, but maybe that's my vision.

"Hu!" I yell up at my window but the man never turns around.

The wind whips my soaking wet hair in my face, blocking my vision for a second.

"Hu! Is that you!" I yell, trying to rip my hair away from my face.

Running back into the house, my towel falls as I climb the stairs but I don't care.

The second I enter my room, the air chills. I can almost see my breath but the window isn't open. No man stands in front of my window but there's a faint scent of faded roses and rain.

"Hugin?"

It almost feels as if the lightest touch brushes against my arm. The hair stands up on my arm and my skin breaks out in goose bumps. My skin feels cool and tingles where I feel him.

I graze my fingers down my skin where I felt his touch, like I could touch him too, if his hand still lingers there.

"Hu, please." My voice breaks. "I miss you so much."

"And I miss you, my Luna."

Closing my eyes, I just want to feel the sensation of him. I swear I feel him brush my hair to the side. *"Forevermore."*

The air is sucked out of the room and feels emptier now.

There's a hollow quiet that seeps through the room, as if a voice had just spoken but was swallowed by silence. I immediately feel his absence.

The sudden ache of melancholy that lingers in my chest, as if his touch seeped into the walls of my heart to let me know how much he misses me too.

"I hate it here without you!" I scream so loud, I feel something shake loose in my chest.

Going into the closet, I pull out one of Hu's old flannels and wrap myself in it.

Walking into my bathroom, I stare at myself in the mirror.

Staring back at me is a ghost. Sunken in cheeks, that are hollowed out. My skin is so pale it's almost luminous. Black impossibly long hair is draped down my back, I pull it forward and put it in a long braid, as I continue to watch my fluid movements. I've always hated my mismatched eyes but Hugin always said it made me look like a mythical creature. Like maybe my one ocean blue eye and my other whiskey brown eye were two souls claiming the same body. One held the weight of oceans, restless and reflective, eternal; while the other was more grounding and steady like the earth. I was never comfortable in my own skin but I was always comfortable in his. Hugin always had this poetic way of making me feel so beautiful when I always just felt like I could crawl into a hole.

Crawling into a hole sounds perfect right about now but I want to make sure I can visit Hu.

Running to our library, I grab Hu's well-loved copy of *Dracula* off of the shelf and my Persephone's Love spells book. I gather my altar bowl and place my rose quartz crystal, some dried rose petals from our garden, and Celtic salt inside of it. Rushing back to the bathroom, I quickly scribe "eternity keeps us entwined" into a small red candle, placing it in the center of the altar bowl. Placing the bowl on top of Hu's copy of *Dracula*, I light the candle. Placing my hand with our ruby ring over my heart, I chant into the mirror over and over again.

"At midnight's hour, when shadows bloom,

I carve your name into my tomb.

By candle's flame and lover's breath,

I summon you, my soul from death.

Blood of rose and wings of night,

Bind your soul to my soul's light.

Through veil of spirits, through parallel doors,

Our bond's eternal, come back to me, be mine once more."

When the candle finally burns out, my eyes catch my bottle of Seroquel sitting on the edge of the tub in the mirror.

Reaching for the bottle, I crack it open. Shaking it, I watch as one pill falls into my hand. Staring at it for a few seconds, I shake the bottle again and three more pills fall out.

Meeting my eyes in the mirror, I throw all four pills into

my mouth and swallow.

"Come back to me, Hu."

15

Hugin

I break the surface, scanning frantically for Eden, but she's nowhere to be seen.

Gulping air, I dive again, letting the sunlight pierce the water to guide me. A glint catches my eye—ten feet down, to the right.

Everything under here is muffled. My heartbeat drums in my ears, loud and relentless.

I kick and swim with everything I've got, closing in on the faint reflection of Eden's wedding ring. She sinks deeper with each second, eyes closed, her body eerily serene. The calmness in her face ignites a raw panic in my chest. I have to save her.

Time races and slows all at once. How long has she been under without air? Too long.

I loop an arm under her, gripping her fragile body, and push toward the surface. Her skin is icy against mine. Light ripples above, mocking our struggle. Fear fuels me, even as my lungs scream and her deadweight drags me down, every stroke feeling like wading through thick honey.

Finally, we break the surface. Relief is fleeting, as I haul her to shore and drop to my knees. Her skin is ghostly pale, lips tinged blue. No heartbeat beneath my fingertips.

"Please...come back to me, baby," I whisper, pumping her chest, then forcing three breaths into her lungs.

Still nothing.

"E! Come back! You can't leave me!" I scream, frantic, starting another round of compressions. One... Two... Three more breaths.

Then a gurgling cough. Eden chokes up water. I roll her onto her side, rubbing her back in slow, soothing circles, heart hammering, praying she'll come fully back to me.

"Baby..." I croak. Feeling like my chest is going to cave in at the thought of almost losing her.

"I'm..." Eden coughs violently, spluttering water from her lips. "I... I'm so sorry, Hu... I don't actually know how to swim."

My heart stutters, disbelief slicing through me. "Wait... What? But you come here all the time, E. You always leave me notes saying, 'gone swimming.'"

She tries to sit up, trembling, but collapses again into my arms. I scoop her close, her soaked body pressed against mine, rubbing her arms up and down, trying to chase away the chill creeping into her skin. The water still drips from her hair, running into my shirt, soaking me, but I don't care.

"Why...aren't you mad at me?" Eden twists, shivering, eyes wide and searching mine.

"My Luna..." I breathe her name like a prayer. "I'm just so relieved you're alive, that you're here, breathing, talking... I can't even think about being mad. I don't even fully understand how you don't know how to swim."

Her lips quiver. "My aunt...never taught me. I love the water...so I come, I sit along the shoreline... I never go out farther than I can stand." She hides her gaze, embarrassment curling her shoulders inward.

I cup her wet chin in my hand, tilting her face toward mine. "I'll teach you, E... I'll teach you to swim. But not today. Today... Today almost took you from me."

Her voice breaks as she whispers, "I know... I know. I didn't realize how fast I would sink. I thought I'd just float back to the top..."

I press my lips softly to hers, tasting the salt of her tears, the fear, the relief. My heartbeat pounds in my chest, in sync with hers. Pulling back, I brush wet strands of hair from her face. "E... I don't care how. I don't care why. I'm just...so damn grateful I got to you in time. That's all that matters. That you came back to me."

Her eyes glimmer, shimmering with water and unshed tears. "I'll always come back to you, Hu. Forevermore."

I pull her into my chest again, holding her tight. The world narrowing to just the warmth of her body in mine and the fact that she's still here. "Forevermore."

16

Eden

Pulling up to the parking lot of Lunalight Lair, I spot Hugin leaning against his truck. Taking him in, as I walk toward him. I notice there's a quiet confidence about him. His white V-neck shirt fits him perfectly, showing the lines of his shoulders, while his black jeans hug his legs in a worn in way. His outfit's complete with black combat boots that almost match mine. His dark hair is perfectly tousled like he's ran his hand through it just enough times and his eyes, those deep dark eyes are watchful and calling to my very soul.

My chest flutters as I walk closer to him. The hum of distant traffic feels almost far away, like the world dimmed its noise just for us.

"Hey," he says, voice calm and warm, like one of my favorite songs.

"Hi," I breathe, smiling despite the nerves tying my stomach into knots.

There is this ease to him, something unspoken that draws me in and it's funny because I never like anyone. I have lived my life as a recluse.

"You hungry?" he asks, breaking the silence.

"Starving."

"I know a great Mediterranean food truck that has the best gyros in town. I thought we could grab some to go and enjoy them by the water," Hugin suggests.

"That sounds perfect."

Hugin opens my door for me. Sliding into his truck, he gently closes the door behind me and I feel the warmth of his interior seep into my skin. The truck smells faintly of leather and a hint of him. We drive in easy silence at first, then conversation flows easy as we talk about movies we both love, our favorite books, and the best concerts we've been to. Hugin makes me laugh until my ribs ache and I'm pretty sure I've never laughed like this in my life.

Time flies and before I know it, we're pulling off the road into a quaint little spot tucked away behind a quiet street. The food truck smells divine as we walk up to the open window. Hugin orders us each a gyro with all the fixins and a few bottles of water.

Grinning, he holds out a gyro for me to take a bite of. The flavors of red onion and tzatziki sauce explode in my mouth. The meat is tender and melts in my mouth. "This might be the best thing I've ever tasted," I groan.

Hugin's eyes are lit up watching me devour my food. "I'm happy you're enjoying it."

Hugin holds his arm out for me toward the car. "Ready?"

"Always." I smile at him.

The drive to the lake is quieter, filled with the soft soundtrack of cicadas and our occasional laughter, as we drive with the windows down through narrow tree-lined roads. The evening air sweeps through the car, whipping my hair all around. My heart feels so full in this moment.

Somewhere in the distance, a loon calls, a melancholy echo that feels like it belongs only to us.

The lake appears on the horizon. The water glimmers under the lavender and fiery orange of the sunset. Waves lap gently against the shoreline, melodic. Hugin spreads a blanket in the soft sand, the grains are cool beneath my bare feet. He pulls out a thermos of hot cocoa and two cups. Pouring each of us a mug and dropping a handful of marshmallows on top, he hands me a mug.

Holding the mug close to me, I savor the smell. The rich chocolate reaches my nose and it's like being wrapped in a comforting hug. "Thank you."

Hugin takes my other hand gently in his and helps me sit on the blanket, pulling another throw out of his basket and draping it over my shoulders.

"Wow... You thought of everything." I smile in awe at how considerate he is.

"I heard that someone wanted a date under the full moon but it gets chilly in the evenings by the water. I just wanted to make sure you were comfortable."

"I am, thank you." If only he knew, I am somehow more comfortable than I've ever been in my life. I have spent my entire life hiding in the shadows of others. Shrinking myself to be palatable. That's why I love working at Lunalight Lair, it's the one place I get to be as wild and free as I'd like to be without consequences.

Hugin sits next to me, savoring the silence. I've never

wanted to just lean into someone before, like I wish to lean into him right now. Words don't have to fill the space. The world is contained in the deep blue hues of the sky, the perfect silver disc mirroring its reflection off the glassy surface of the water, and the way his shoulder occasionally brushes mine.

The edges of the lake are shadowed, trees standing as silent as silhouettes, their branches swaying gently in the night breeze. I feel myself almost swaying with them. I'm so relaxed right now.

The moonlight spills over everything, creating an almost otherworldly glow. My breath catches in my throat when my eyes leave the moon and are magnetized to Hugin's. I think the world itself might be holding its breath beneath his gaze.

Hugin stands, extending his hand out to me. "Dance with me?"

I laugh softly, caught off guard by the sudden intimacy of the moment. "Here? There's no music."

"Here," he says, pulling me gently to my feet. "If I had to wait this long to know you. The world can wait."

Barefoot in the sand, Hugin holds me close, as we sway together, slow and easy. The waves whisper around us, the wind tousles our hair, and the moon full and luminous, spills across the water. Its reflection illuminates his face, the curve of his smile, the sharp shadows of his cheekbones, and the quiet awe in his eyes as he looks at me, as if I am something precious.

I press my cheek to his chest, feeling the steady beat of his heart against mine. My heart beat steadying in his arms. Hugin tilts my chin up and our eyes meet. It's like every fiber in my being is reaching for him, and him for me, as if maybe our souls recognize each other. As if maybe, we met in a past life.

"Hu..." I whisper, almost involuntarily.

"E..." His voice is soft, reverent, carrying the weight of something unspoken but undeniable. Something too soon to give a name to but also not soon enough.

We sway slowly, nature our music of the night. The waves, the wind, the rustle of leaves, blending with our very own rhythm. The world around us fades. I feel as if we have been orbiting toward this moment all of our lives. Two stars colliding at last.

Then, finally, our lips meet. Soft, tentative at first, then deeper, a kiss that feels like home in its purest form. Every unspoken thought, every missed heartbeat, every instant that had led us here crystallized in this kiss. Two lost stars, finding their only lights.

The moon hangs high above us, casting its silver light over the water, the sand, and us. We pull back slightly, foreheads touching, breaths mingling.

"I'll always come back to you," Hugin murmurs.

"Forevermore," I whisper, and it feels like the first and the last truth I will ever need.

A caw, has us both looking up, a lone black crow, wings spanned out wide, flies like a shadow across the light of the full moon before it disappears into the dark sky.

Hugin gently places his hand over the ruby ring dangling around his neck. Our eyes meet, and in that fleeting look, we silently know.

We stay there on the shoreline, under the full moon, wrapped in each other's arms. His light and my dark dance as if we are two separate flames burning perfectly in harmony, never wanting to engulf the other. The capacity of love that exists between us, feels as if we were created from the same source. The water glitters like scattered stars, dancing to their own rhythm of the night, knowing somehow, unshakably, we found something that would last a lifetime.

17

Hugin

Eden paces the hospital room like a caged animal. I watch her from the corner of the room, the air between us trembling with an invisible weight. I have no voice. No touch, only the faintest hum of presence.

I watch as goose bumps pebble her skin the closer I get to her. Eden shivers, rubbing her hands up and down her arms to ward off the chill.

"I'm coming back for you, Eden Orion. I'm coming back," I whisper, but she can no longer perceive my being.

A knock on the door has Eden halting in her tracks. "Come in." Her voice is as lifeless as I am.

Nurse Iris walks in. "Mrs. Orion, we've set up transportation home for you. The driver will be here in ten minutes. Here are the belongings the police acquired from your vehicle at the scene." The nurse hands Eden two duffel bags, one mine and one hers.

Eden hesitates for just a moment before taking them both from her. "Thank you."

"Here is your medication. The Seroquel is to be taken once before bed. Make sure you take this no earlier than thirty minutes before you are ready to go to sleep. Do not operate a vehicle or drink alcohol with these. They can make you incredibly drowsy. We've arranged for a psychiatrist who will come to your home to evaluate you once a month to make sure you are still doing well with your medication and do not require any adjustments."

"Do I actually need to take this?"

"The short answer is yes. The real answer is you experienced a very traumatic event, Eden. Seroquel helps with the insomnia you've been experiencing since the accident. It can help dull your reaction to any nightmares or flashbacks you may encounter. It can even help stabilize your mood and any restlessness you are feeling. It isn't our first line of treatment for grief itself, but it is for severe insomnia, depression, and trauma-related conditions."

"Okay," Eden says, defeated.

"We only want to help you, Mrs. Orion," Nurse Iris states, before her phone rings.

She answers and thanks whoever she is talking to. "Your ride is here."

Eden takes her bottle of antipsychotics from Nurse Iris and unzips her duffel bag, placing it on the top of her clothes and zipping it closed. "Thank you for your kindness while I've been here." She struggles to make eye contact with her.

Nurse Iris pulls Eden into a hug, that seems to startle Eden at first but then she softens into it. "Please reach out if you need anything. I cannot imagine how you are feeling. You will be in my thoughts, Mrs. Orion."

I notice Eden squeezes her a little bit tighter before finally releasing her, grabbing the duffel bags and walking toward the door of her hospital room.

Eden looks back into the corner of the room, one last time, where I've been standing keeping a watchful eye on her. Her eyes meet mine for just a moment before she walks out.

"I'm coming back, E. Our love is tethered by something more stubborn than death."

*E*den sits in the living room; her body pressed against the couch as if gravity alone is the only thing anchoring her. She stares off at the fireplace, but there is no fire, no warmth in this house. It is a constant chill. The house is silent aside from the soft hum of the refrigerator and the faint sigh that feels like it comes from the house.

Eden's eyes are wide but unfocused. Almost like she's in a trance. Staring at nothing and yet in that nothing, I see the fracture of her soul. It's as if her body is here, her heart still beating, pumping blood through her veins, her lungs still breathing. But every other piece of her is gone from the world of the living in every way that matters.

It has been four months since the accident. Four months since I drove into the dark, leaving her behind a shell of who I know her to be. Four months since I traded my soul for hers, hoping Eden would go on living for the both of us. I remember the final helpless thought I would never be able to hold her again. And now, I can only watch as the woman who is everything to me dissolves into silence.

I try to move closer, to whisper her name. "Eden," I breathe into the empty space, but my words fall flat. The living cannot hear me. The world is muted to my presence, and yet I can feel every tremor of her grief as if it were my own heartbeat, a drum of sorrow that will never cease.

Eden's eyes flicker sometimes, like tiny stars struggling to pierce a night that will not end. I watch as her hands twitch, fingers brushing against the fabric of the couch as if trying to grasp something, anything. But it isn't me she reaches for. It isn't anything at all. Just emptiness.

When the doctor arrives, she is distant and compliant, her words are hollow. She accepts the medication refill. Her bottle always empty. He encourages her to rest, to sleep, to forget. But I know she is not forgetting. Sleep is not her refuge. I watch her toss and turn at night. Screaming violently into the dark. Her screams piercing even the hollowest parts of me.

The medication dulls her, softens the jagged edges of reality, but it cannot mend the chasm inside of her. I hover, watching her every move. My heart aching in a way that no spirit should feel. I watch her drift in and out of the fog, the shortest thread between sanity and collapse.

$\mathcal{M}$aybe grief isn't grief at all, maybe it's possession.

There are nights like tonight, when her grief becomes too heavy even for the antipsychotics. I watch her suddenly flinch, her body jerking as though shadows themselves are assaulting her in her sleep. "No...no, he's not gone..." she would whisper, trembling. Tears streaming down her ghostly cheeks.

I lay wrapped around her, silently crying with her. Wishing she could feel me hold her close to me. Trying to melt into her so she can feel that she isn't alone. That I'm still here, tethered invisibly, eternally to her.

*E*den paces our room in the dead of night. Muttering my name over and over again like a prayer, as if she could manifest my return if she said it enough. If she pleads for me enough. I can hear her mind screaming, a storm of memories and guilt and impossible what-ifs that no one could see. I wish I could make her understand this isn't her fault. That I died for her and I wouldn't have done anything differently.

Every single day, from sun up to sun down, I watch Eden live like a ghost. I watch her slump against the walls of this house, the bed in our room, the floor of the tub, as if gravity itself is the only thing keeping her tethered to life. Some days she makes it outside. Robotically tending to the garden. Speaking to the roses as if they'll give her life. I curse, softly, desperately, this cruel twist of fate that left me alive in spirit, and her trapped in a body that could no longer carry the weight of her own heart.

Some nights, when it seems as if the medication is helping carry some of the weight and she sleeps fitfully, I lay closer to her. I brush my fingers through her hair, tracing the line of her cheeks, that are as hollowed out as my chest cavity. I whisper promises to her that I can no longer make.

Laying here unseen, unheard, a guardian of her grief, a shadow of her love, hoping that she will never forget me and the essence of our bond that not even death could sever.

Because even in the darkness, even in the grief, even in the moments that tear her mind apart and leave her soul feeling untethered, I know one thing.

She is still Eden. She is still mine. And I will not leave her, not even in death.

18

Eden

The candle has long since burned out, yet I remain on the bathroom floor, staring at the envelope in my hands. Its edges are softened and muted from being pressed beneath this book.

It took me months after returning from the hospital to even touch Hugin's duffel bag. It felt like a betrayal to put his things away, knowing he would never wear them again. Even his copy of *Dracula* went back to its usual place on our library shelves, as if the act could somehow preserve him.

This envelope, how had I never noticed it before? Perhaps it had been so carefully tucked away, or perhaps I had been lost in a fog too thick to see.

I brush my fingertips over the 'HO' monogram, pressed into a perfect disc of crimson wax.

When did you write this, Hu?

Breaking the seal, I lift the folded paper from the envelope. My hands shake. A small white card slips to the floor, but I do not reach for it. Because the moment my eyes land on his handwriting, a sob escapes my chest.

I trace the flowing calligraphy with my fingers, memorizing each curve and line like braille, engraving him into my memory one stroke at a time.

'My Beloved Eden,
There are moments in life that feel ordinary, until you step into them and then everything just shifts. Being haunted by you was one of those moments. From the instant our eyes met, I knew I'd been waiting for you forever. I felt a truth deeper than words could convey. That maybe our souls had been waiting for each other long before we even knew the other existed.

Every day since has been a story not even my wildest dreams could have conjured and now, I cannot imagine living a single moment without you. Your essence, your touch, the way your presence feels like home. I became your compass, but you became my shelter. Your darkness holds mine without flinching, while my light keeps your shadows at bay. I carry you with me, always, as if our hearts were woven together by threads spun from fate herself.

On this anniversary, I want to remind you that our love is endless, boundless, and unshakeable. As the water signs are bound to the moon, so is my love for you; eternal in the tides, ever flowing, infinite in its depth. You and I are fated, my Luna.

Eden, you are my destiny, my purpose, my always. My heart will always find its way to you, eternally. I am forever yours. Forevermore,
Hugin'

The words are blurred from the tears rimming my eyes. I read the letter over and over again until I can't possibly keep my eyes open anymore.

A loud crashing sound has my eyes flying open. My head feels heavy, fuzzy. Pushing myself up off the bathroom floor, I stumble into the vanity before making my way out the door.

The sound of shattering glass has me sprinting down the hall. My head screams at the sudden movement.

"Hu!"

When I make it to the door of the library, the lamp from Hu's desk is shattered in pieces on the floor. A crow sits on a stack of cards sitting on top of the desk.

"Forevermore," it caws, eyes dark as midnight meeting mine. It studies me as I walk slowly toward it.

"What did you just say!" I dive for the crow, but it's much quicker than I am. It spreads its wings and flies above my head, going to the peak of the cathedral ceilings.

But not before its feet knock several cards onto the floor.

"Forevermore," the crow caws again.

"Stop saying that!" I scream.

The crow makes a quick exit out of the room, flying through the open door, down the hall and stairwell.

"Get back here!" My feet thunder down the stairs after it.

It caws again and then swoops under the doorframe, flying out my back door. Which was already wide open. I run toward it, but it's already out of sight by the time I get outside.

Running back upstairs, I walk into the library. Broken glass litters the floor. I sit cross-legged next to the shattered glass. Dim light trickles in from the one lone window behind me.

My deck of tarot cards sits askew on the desk, but three lone cards lie perfectly face down on the floor amongst the broken glass.

My cards are worn at the edges from years of use. Hugin used to let me give him readings all the time. Their energy is familiar to me, almost intimate. But I have not touched these since before the accident, fearful for what they might whisper back. It seems the crow wants me to know something though. Hesitantly I reach for the card closest to me. My breath trembles.

Do I even need to ask them a question? Has the crow already asked for me?

Three cards already chosen. Past, Present, Future. Awaiting my fate.

"What awaits me?" My thoughts whisper.

My stomach clenches, as I stare at the lightning struck spine, people falling helplessly into the abyss. The Tower— collapse. Squeezing the card tightly in my hand, I shake off the unease. The memory of the hospital walls closing in on me. Dr. Edgar telling me Hugin was pronounced dead at the scene. This card didn't need an explanation. I had already lived the worst thing that could happen to me.

If these cards are going to be brutal, I need something to take the edge off. Stepping through the broken glass, I walk with blood-stained feet to my kitchen. Pulling open every cabinet until I find my last three bottles of red wine. It feels almost poetic, that I have three cards to read and three bottles of wine left. I don't even bother grabbing a glass, simply popping the cork and then taking a long gulp.

The bottle dangles between two fingers as I climb back up the spiral staircase. Walking back into the library, I lie on the floor staring up at the ceiling, and reach for the next card closest to me.

My breath hitches when my eyes catch the goat-headed figure's eyes staring back into mine, chains coiled around the neck of its captives. I feel like a captive to my own mind. I'm bringing the bottle of wine to mouth, when it registers that The Devil card also means addiction.

My throat tightens, body going rigid at the thought of the pills I take to sleep. The wine that I drink to dull the edges of this grief. The empty hours I spend not knowing if I'm asleep or awake. These demons inside me, weaving their chains tighter and tighter, and still each day I exist, just continuously living in this hell.

My fingers find a shard of broken glass before I find the third card. I let the sharp edges dig in just a bit, to remind me I am awake and not dreaming in this moment.

Heart hammering in my head, I turn over the final card. I can feel the card before I even see it, my stomach twisting in knots. Usually, the skeleton riding on a skeleton horse means rebirth, change, even transformation, but for me. I could feel it in my very bones, that the Death card actually meant the death of me.

The caw from the crow is a warning. A cold, merciless warning. The Tower. The Devil. Death.

If I did not turn from the path I was on, my fate would be sealed. Just as that letter had been for two years.

Dark wings block the light of the library, casting shadows in every corner. A chill racks through my body. For a moment I swear I feel a hand brush my shoulder, cool yet invisible.

"Hu?"

Nothing but silence. Is my mind unraveling?

My eyes find the cards again; my chest constricts as if someone was tightening a noose around my neck. I can hear my own breath, shallow and quick, like a bird beating against a cage.

"No..." I whisper. Shaking my head violently. "No, I will not..."

But the cards lay there laughing at me, their message already etched into my fate.

19

Hugin

The room is heavy with silence as I linger at Eden's bedside. I was almost surprised when she scraped herself off the floor of the library, after seeing the cards I had left. Eden was nothing short of stubborn the eleven years we spent together. Seeing her wither away to nothing because of me has left me more shadow than flesh.

She always took her tarot readings to heart. Certain the universe was guiding her through the ups and downs of life. I know with certainty that Eden will die, if she doesn't find a way out of the void. Getting her to use her cards again was the only way I could think of to shine some light on that.

I lean close to her, whispering her name with a tenderness that stirs only the faintest flicker in her breathing. My hand, translucent, hovers above her hand, willing her to wake. Willing her to follow me, to see what waits beyond the door. The memorial card lies in the bathroom where it fell out of the letter I wrote to her two days before the accident.

The card is the last fragile tether between us. I ache with desperation for her to notice it before it's too late.

Eden was not supposed to become my afterlife.

20

Eden

Some nights, I swear I feel his hand in mine. Mourning shouldn't feel this much like love.

The storm begins like a murmur against the windows.

They say love doesn't survive death, but why does he keep finding me in every shadow?

I rise, feeling a presence in this room, as if I'm being watched with careful eyes. "Hu?"

Shadows dance along the walls of my room, as lightning flashes in the distance outside.

My feet slide from beneath the sheets of my bed. The world outside becoming a chorus of fury from the storm. Rain clatters against the glass, thunder shaking the frame of the house, and trees bend to their will, as if kneeling for the gods.

But I don't hear a thing. In the soft blankness of my sleepwalking mind, I hear only his voice.

Hugin.

His voice threads through my dream pulling me close,

as if he's on the other end of the invisible string. Leading me down the hallway barefoot, dressed in only my nightgown. The back door shrieks open as if the house is trying to sound an alarm for me to wake up. As if Hugin's ghost is reluctant to release me. And yet, I still walk through the door without hesitation.

The night consumes me all at once. Wind claws at my hair, tangling it across my face. The rain is razor sharp and ice cold, my nightgown clings against my skin, until I can barely feel the line between skin and becoming the storm.

Still I walk until I tear off running into the night. My bare feet slap against wet earth, slipping on roots, stumbling over stones.

"Hugin!" I yell, spotting him in the distance. A white shape, a glimmer of presence between the black tree trunks, just up ahead.

"Hugin! Wait!" My voice cracks, lost in the wind.

The forest comes alive with more than wind. A cry splits through the storm, rasping, commanding. The crow.

It swoops low, a streak of black against even darker night. Its wings slick and heavy with rainfall.

It comes from my left side, close enough that I feel the beat of its feathers against my cheek. Startled, I flinch, but keep running, convinced it was just a shadow.

The crow circles back around, diving again, cawing out, as though demanding I turn back.

But I can't.

Hugin.

A flicker of pale skin in the trees, a hand reaching out. "Come back to me, E." His voice reverberates throughout the trees, piercing my very soul. I see him again, just a glimmer.

My lungs are on fire, my nightgown is plastered to my legs, my hair a wild mess. And yet I run harder.

The forest moans and groans with the storm. Dark shadows everywhere I turn. A crack like the sky itself is breaking open, along with my heart, tears through the sky. And a tree, that has likely stood the test of time, splits straight down the center. It's almost as if the world is splintering like I am, in real time.

I barely have time to see the tree falling. I hurl myself forward, mud splattering, a scream tearing free from my throat and still I linger in a space where my mind is still dreaming, yet my body is moving as if it's awake. The tree crashes down behind me with a roar that seems to swallow the entire world whole. Bark and leaves burst into the air like shrapnel.

My legs are pumping of their own accord. Muscle memory.

I don't look back.

The crow catches up to me again. The speed of my legs seeming to pump fury through its veins. It screams again, swooping at my head, brushing my shoulder with its wing as though it could physically change the direction of the path I'm on.

I stumble, trip, and catch myself on a tree, before I continue to run forward.

My chest heaves, the cold restricting every breath I try to take.

Suddenly, the forest breaks.

The shoreline stretches out before me, a hollow of

darkness where the trees give way to sand and rock. The storm churns the lake into a thing of teeth. And an island that breathes, is an island that eats. Waves gnash against the shore, the spray dissolving into the air and mingling with the rain. The storm seems to close in on me, sealing me into this pocket of darkness.

My foot strikes something solid. A root? A stone? I can't see. I pitch forward, my body hitting the sand hard, my skull striking something unyielding beneath me. White explodes across my eyes.

I'm met with silence.

The last thing I hear, the crow crying into the storm.

21

Eden

The impact reverberates through my skull like a bell struck in the dark. For a moment, I just lay stunned in the wet sand of the shoreline. My breath ragged. My palms sink into the soaked sand, fingers clawing, as if I could anchor myself to the earth but the water is already rushing close, spilling froth around my wrists.

I try to push myself up, but it's no use. My body trembles, my arms and legs aching from exhaustion, cold, and the heaviness of the rain clinging to my nightgown.

The lake exhales with the storm, a wave surging higher than normal. The wave sweeps over my chest. It reaches my soaking hair, and then I'm choking on water. I cough and try to roll to my side, only for another wave to slap against my face again.

My breath catches wrong. I swallow more than I can cough out. Water fills my throat, invading my lungs, the weight of it clinging even after the wave has receded. I roll onto my back, chest heaving, eyes open to the stormy sky. Rain lashes my face like tiny needles.

It wasn't supposed to be this way. I was only trying to get back to you, Hu.

I know I saw him. Wasn't that his shape out there, walking just beyond the waves?

A male figure beckoning me closer?

I reach out my hand, fingers splayed. My lips move, soundless, trying to form his name.

My chest convulses. I cough violently, a wet, tearing sound, but each cough draws the water deeper. My vision blurs. Black ink bleeds into the edges of the world.

And then, flashes.

They come like lightning, violent, searing, and impossible to look away from.

I see myself in black, my face gaunt beneath a veil. I stand before Hugin's headstone, but I am not the only one there. Mourners stand scattered like shadows among the graves, and another headstone lays beside his, fresh, the earth still raw. Kaia Odin etched there.

It couldn't be. I stagger back in the vision, but the ground opens up. I see the grave swallowing me as my small casket descends. The air is heavy with the smell of lilies. Thunder rolls above. In the distance, another stone bears the name of Hugin's mother, the date of death, the same as mine.

My death twined with hers.

A sob catches in my throat or maybe it's just another cough. I claw at my chest, desperate for air, but all I feel is heaviness. Water sloshing where air should be.

I'm dying again...I think before the vision shifts.

I'm following Hugin, just as I followed him tonight,

except this time he isn't a shadow among the trees, but a boy of flesh and bone. I drift after him, sometimes seen, sometimes unseen. The gift of being able to see the other world as a child, the veil still open.

I feel this unexplainable pull toward Hugin. My steps silent, my presence more shadow than body. I watch him sit under the tree at the cemetery, melancholy surrounding him like a haze, as he watches his father talk to his mother's headstone. His sadness fills my chest and all I want to do is take it away.

Walking with him to his car, I see my mom—Kaia's mom—crying in my father's arms. Her friends whisper that they can't believe my parents didn't lock the gate of the pool, since I didn't know how to swim. That it's so tragic to lose a child at just three years old.

So fixated on Hugin though, I continue to walk past them and join him in his car on his return home from the graveside. His shoulders are slumped, I feel his heart aching and I feel myself clinging, tethered, unwilling to let him go.

His room is dimly lit, glow in the dark stars placed all over his ceiling, in his childhood room. Hugin lies asleep, covers pulled over his small frame as he softly whimpers in his sleep. On his nightstand lies two cards, his mother's memorial card and mine. When he thought he dropped his mom's memorial card in the cemetery, he actually picked up one of mine. Our faces are two portraits of absence, side by side, close enough that the edges touch. I feel myself gravitate toward him, wanting to wrap him in the delicate lace of my light, and nest in the grief he can't put down.

In that moment, the world pulled at me in two directions, one toward the grave, deep and final, where my body would sleep beneath lilies. Another toward something vast and formless, a current-like tide urging me forward. Rebirth.

The way that my soul called to Hugin's only allowed me the one choice. Naïve to the consequences of what being reborn in another body would mean.

Another vision flashes.

My mother in a hospital room, pale and trembling, as my cry pierces the dimly lit room. She manages a fleeting smile at the sound before her strength gives way, her hand slipping from the midwife's grasp.

"She's hemorrhaging! Grab me a crash cart!" the midwife screams, pulling the alarm for a code blue. Alarms blare as my mother's heartbeat drops, a few moments after a life was given, one was taken. My mother's chest goes still; her gaze fixed on nothing. As I lie swaddled and wailing in a nurse's arms. The universe demanding balance. No soul can enter without another leaving. My mother's death becoming the gateway that made space for my rebirth. Entering the world with no parent, only the echo of a love that ended the moment it began.

My head screams as another vision violently crashes through me.

My body hanging upside down lifeless, only held in place by my seat belt, in Hugin's truck. Hugin's face looks over toward me, begging a crow to save me, as if the crow were the reaper himself. I understood in that moment he had given his life for me, swapping his very thread for mine in that split second where worlds collided.

Hugin hears a loud cry from the crow, but I hear his mother's voice, a distant memory from another lifetime, a cry from her that breaks my own heart. "I wish I could save you too, my sweet boy."

She and I died the same day, but she lingered as a quiet crow in a tree, as I danced in spirit around her son to try to soften the pain at the loss of her. Her essence of love flowing through our lifeblood within her heirloom ruby ring that ties us as family.

My lips tremble with words I cannot form. My lungs scream for air that does not come.

The water has already taken me, for the second time in my lifetimes.

But the visions will not let me go. I realize in this moment this is what they must mean when they say your life flashes before your eyes as you lay dying.

22

Eden

Time no longer flowed the same once the water claimed me. The perfect exit for a Pisces, taken by the element from which I was born.

At first, I didn't even realize I was gone. My body slipped beneath the storm, yet I clung stubbornly to Hugin.

Eventually, my presence, weightless but insistent, found its way back to our house. The first thing I noticed was his mother's ruby ring, lying in my altar bowl on the bathroom sink. Relief washed through me; I hadn't lost it near the lake. My gaze fell to the floor, where one lone tarot card, The Lovers lay upright, next to the anniversary letter from Hugin and the memorial card of Kaia Odin. One ocean-blue eye and one chocolate-brown stare back at me, matching my own mismatched gaze. Hugin must've known all along. For the soul lingers in the eyes, unchanging. Two souls reincarnated may not recognize each other's faces but their eyes will always give them away. And my eyes have forever remained the same, no matter what lifetime I exist in.

Grief seemed to stretch across the void, tethering two souls as if time itself were nothing but illusion. I hovered like a shadow, one day bleeding into the next, waiting for Hugin, but he never came. The silence of his absence weighed heavier than life ever had. Days dissolved into weeks, weeks into months, yet the air remained still. He was gone, utterly absent.

In that darkness, my soul, tired, broken, and aching, reached blindly for a tether, a solace I barely understood. And yet, Hu had already accepted it, all those years ago. Our souls had entwined in a pattern older than stars, looping endlessly. Grief would draw us together. Love would hold us. Loss could never sever our bond. Each life, each incarnation, was another chance to recognize one another, to ache, to remember.

I decided, then, that it was time.

*T*he darkness was not empty. It pressed against me, thick and velvety, a womb enclosing me as if I were a caterpillar in a cocoon.

I felt myself unravel first at the edges. The delicate threads of my being loosening, slipping through my fingers. I tried to hold myself together, but the silk dissolved into a current, carrying me forward into the unknown.

Then, gently, piece by piece, something stitched me back together, but not as I had been. I was no longer the woman who chased shadows through storm-bent trees. I was something new.

Life pulsed through my veins, a rhythm that defied naming. The water that had drowned me. The storm that had claimed me. The crow that had become my only friend. All were wiped from memory, yet tucked deep into my marrow, lessons of the past I carried still.

I opened my eyes to blackness. I saw nothing, yet I felt more alive than ever. My first breath came heavy with all I had ever loved and lost.

Hugin's presence lingered, not as a choice, not as fleeting desire, but as an eternal certainty. His soul would call to mine when he was ready. And I would be here, waiting, as I always had been.

Epilogue

Eden

Rebirth came as sensation first. The warmth of new blood coursing through me. The ache of forming bones. The slow unfurling of wings. Consciousness stirred like petals opening beneath an eclipse, fragile and deliberate.

My heart begins to beat again, and I feel Hugin's pulse echoing within me. We are inevitable, after all.

When the first light seeps through the trees, I find myself surrounded by a misty forest. The air carries the scent of rainfall and freshly blooming roses. Darkness still lingers at the edges of my vision as my eyes flutter open.

I am perched upon a stone in a garden of red roses when something shiny falls from the sky into a rain puddle at my feet. Looking up, I see a crow circling in the pale dawn light. Every glide, every dive, is a performance, a dance of purpose. It lands beside me, tilting its head as if assessing, waiting… A strange familiarity settles in my chest.

The crow hops into the garden, seizes something in its beak, and returns to the stone. Nestling close, it offers me a red ruby ring.

As I go to reach for it, I catch my reflection in the

puddle. Twisting to meet the crow's gaze, it caws softly, "Forevermore."

I rise and fly toward the crow, startled by this revelation, only to notice the headstone beneath it: *Hugin Orion + Eden Orion, eternity keeps us entwined.*

"It was always you. You came back." A conversation, in a language only we know.

"I promised you, I would find you in every lifetime, E. Life and death, it's you, baby," Hugin declares.

Together, our black wings unfurl, spanning the sky as we soar toward the old oak in our backyard. Our love is quiet but fierce, stitched into every glance, every playful chase through the clouds, an eternal bond that cannot be broken.

In every lifetime, I will be his, and he will be mine. Always. Forevermore.

Acknowledgments

Kenzie, thank you for your outpouring of support and love of my work. Your excitement has been contagious from the beginning. This cover you created is an absolute dream come true. I am so grateful to you for becoming my PA and helping create our epic street team and gorgeous graphics for my books! I adore you! @kenziekillswitch

Rach, thank you for being the best seester, greatest supporter, and helping me brainstorm my crazy ideas. As well as asking the best questions to make sure everything flows as it should. I love you to pieces.

Holly, thank you for letting me bounce ideas off of you at work, helping me word things until they're perfect, and making sure everything works in the organized chaos that it is. I owe you ten PSL's. Love you!

Mum, thank you for reading and rereading my manuscripts, every single one of them. Thank you for being here for me and supporting my work. I love you!

To Cleo, thank you so much for working with me and dealing with my impulsivity. For creating such beautiful formatting that flows so beautifully inside, as you always do! I look forward to working with you on many more projects! @devotedpages_designs

To my editors Darlene and Athena, thank you for working so hard to make this flow smoothly and dealing with my impulsivity! You have been amazing to work with! I look forward to working on other projects with you in the future! @sistersgetlit.erary

Seth and Allie thank you so much for helping bring my

cover photo to life and seeing my vision!

To the rest of my family, friends, street team, and fellow readers thank you so much for your support and outpouring of love. This dream wouldn't be a reality without all of you. I love you more than you know!

This story was a way for me to process losing the greatest love of my life. I hope that it finds those who need it when they meet grief in their life. I hope you can feel comforted by the possibility that we may always meet again in another life.

About the Author

Britt Reign is a dog mom, healthcare worker, and writer.

Music obsessed. A tarot/oracle reader. Avid book and poetry reader and audiobook listener.

She grew up in the suburbs of Pittsburgh, Pennsylvania and currently resides near the mountains in West Virginia. Her soul however, is yearning to be by the sea.

She has a love for travel and the beauty that surrounds us in everyday life.

Britt Reign has also published a love triangle romance, Chokehold, Bloodsport under pen name Britt Reign. @brittreignauthor

Book blog: @waggingwithwords